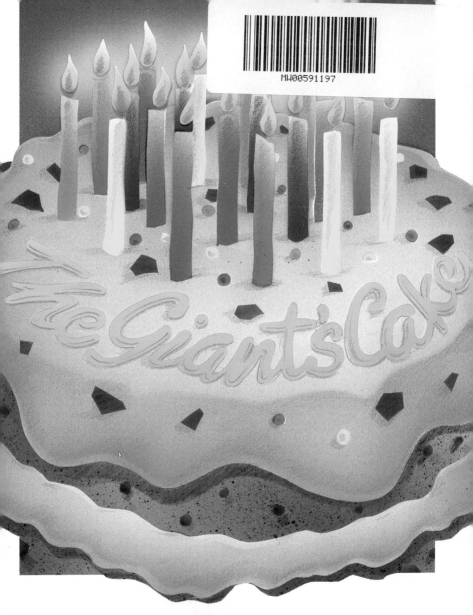

The Giant's Cake

It was the giant's birthday.
He lit the candles on top of
his giant birthday cake,
and blew.

The candles wouldn't blow ou
So he blew even harder.

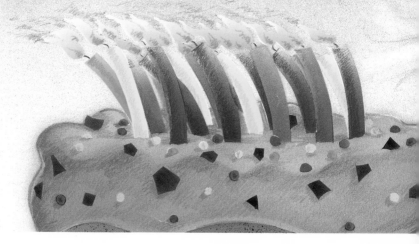

3

WHOOOOOO!
He blew the pirate ship
out to sea.
Whoosh! Whoosh! Whoosh!
The pirate's parrot was scared.

5

WHOOOOOO!
He blew the apples
off the trees.
Plop, plop, plop,
and down the road
they rolled.

6

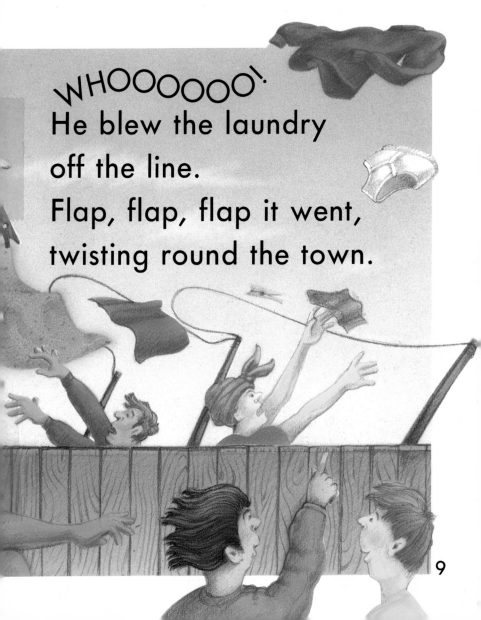

WHOOOOOO!
He blew the laundry
off the line.
Flap, flap, flap it went,
twisting round the town.

9

WHOOOOOO!
He blew parked cars
down the road.
Bang, crash, smash
they went!

10

WHOOOOOO!
He blew all the people
down the street.
Higglety, pigglety,
rumble, tumble,
rumpity, bumpity, BUMP!

"That giant is a nuisance!"
the people said.

By now all the candles
were blown out.
"Happy Birthday to me,"
said the giant.

Then he said to the people,
"I'll give you some cake."
So he cut a giant-sized slice..

and put it in the park.
And everyone had cake
for a week!

16